You Meet No Strangers

by

Sara Fryd

also
by Sara Fryd

What If... only one child remained?
The Coincidental Cricket
Woodruff the Chili Dog
Little Girls and Purple Cats
A Painter's Daughter

Copyright © 2011 by Sara Fryd
ISBN-13: 978-0615450155
ISBN-10: 0615450156

Sara Arizona LLC ~ http://sara-arizona.com ~ 520.909.0270

for...

...the 260,000 readers of every nationality, race, and religion that live in 188 countries who have come by to read my blog.

Thank you for making my dreams come true.

ACKNOWLEDGMENTS

For Fae Talisman, a redhead with a view, who saw the potential redhead in an unsure girl child who wanted desperately to become an independent woman. For "Judy" Judith Westerfield, a brunette, who became a flashlight in my hand lighting my way. For Howard Weiske, a blond, who taught me I painted with words and when I learned to trust the universe enough to share my words, tossing them to the wind, I would no longer be afraid. For Edith Kroschel, who thanked me for seeing past her wrinkles and read my poems to her swim class. For Clara Peck Schultz, who made me read my poems out loud again and again to her on the telephone, reminding me to stay in the present. For Chikita Davis, a beautiful human being, who saw through me on Waikiki Beach and ultimately wound up naming this book. And to Alex Zola, my cousin, whose courage to look at himself and his relationships in the written format of stories, gave me the courage to look at mine. Truly amazing how the puzzle pieces of one's life begin to fit together when they can be seen on paper in a black and white.

CONTENTS

1. PISH IN DIEN HOSEN

It's easy to love people who love you back. Who are good, kind, and remember your birthday. Loving someone who is a pain in the behind is much harder. And yet, somehow much more memorable and educational. Humans seem to need everything to be exceedingly problematic to learn anything, and I am no exception. Neither was Aron.

Aron was Nusha's (my Mother's) youngest sibling and we were raised together till I was almost six. We were Jewish refugees living in difficult circumstances outside Munich in 1948. His challenge wasn't necessarily that he was a Holocaust survivor; Aron would have been a problem child even if he had been born in Des Moines. He had this "j'ne sais quois" quality of intelligence, Dean Martin good looks, and the ability to charm anyone he wanted to. The operative word here is "wanted," but those stories will have to wait for another 4 a.m. morning.

He took crap from no one! Certainly not one three-year-old girl with a big Polish Ghetto Litvak accented Yiddish/German mouth that knew as many languages as she was old. Thanks to a liberated Father, she had her own Rabbi Hebrew tutor at two and learning Yiddish on purpose to figure out what the grown-ups were saying was a piece of cake. Has to be the Zaslover Chutzpah genes we are so well-known for.

Nusha liked nicknames and everyone's had a little twang of some sort. She called him "Aronchik" – the Romania, Russian, Polish, German, French, Yiddish (all languages she was fluent in) equivalent of Aron. She also made him take care of me.

Eighteen-year-old males don't much like babysitting their bratty nieces, even if they are adorably cute with blond curly locks. So here I am toilet trained, needing to go to the bathroom, pulling on his trouser leg.

"Aronchik," I cried. "Ich daf gehen pishen." (Aron, I have to go pee.)

"Pish in dien hosen," my uncle responded. (Pee in your trousers.)

"Pish auf sich" I answered. (Pee on yourself.)

Great practice for succeeding in law school. Don't you think?

2. BENNY

Munich was always cold, especially in 1946. We lived in a "lager" – an American Displaced Person's Camp. A four-story building with large rooms that housed multiple individuals and families. Eighty people to a room, each group divided by hanging dark khaki Army blankets. This community home with no privacy, and Army folding cots for beds, is where I spent my formative years. The Jews' Holocaust was over. America had won World War II. Mine was just beginning.

On top of the mountain near the building, the train ran by every night. Even with my eyes closed covered by the dark olive blanket; I could always hear the whistle. Every time I heard the sound, I was afraid - afraid that it would come and take my Papa away. I'd hear them whispering in Yiddish at night when they thought I was sleeping. My American Army bed was only inches away.

By current standards, Papa was small in stature, standing only 5' 2" tall. Telly Savalas' twin brother and half his height. Though to me he had all the strength and charm of Kojak.

The highest safest place I've ever known were his shoulders when I was three and Simchat Torah was taking place autumn of 1948. Outside we walked to a makeshift synagogue down rolling green hills. He held my little legs tight just above my shoes and socks. I felt so warm, loved, and very tall. In my right hand was a wooden pole holding a white Israeli flag with blue stripes, a blue Star of David, and a little red apple at the top. My left hand clung to his ear and held on to his baldhead for dear life. All together we were over seven feet tall my papa, the flag, and me.

By then the Allies had won the War and Jewish children could walk the icy blood drenched soil of Germany without being carted off in trucks like strays picked up by dog catchers. By the time I was four, I had my own rabbinical tutor, an old white-haired bearded Orthodox rabbi who taught me Hebrew. The Women's Liberation Movement wouldn't come into existence for another twenty years, though it mattered not to my Papa that I was only a girl. He cared that I love the process of learning, of reading the ancient text. He wanted to make sure that I learned the alphabet of my dead grandparents (who disappeared with a heartbeat when a German bomb exploded their building in the Warsaw Ghetto). He made sure he gave me the gift of going to school; something he dreamed of but never had the chance.

Papa was an expert in the "black market" and came down the hill of our makeshift town in a pale tan Mercedes Benz sedan with sunroof and matching leather seats. We never did find out how he "bought it." He pulled up along side the building with the sunroof open and me in the back seat, while my other threw wrapped candy from the window above. I can close my eyes and still hear the laughter.

With all the horrors he experienced, I remember him smiling and joyous, always full of stories and singing. Always singing me to sleep. *"Avf daem pripichok brent a firerl. In de shteeb is heis. Un de Rebbe layrent kliene kinderlech daem aleph baze..."* - *"On the hearth there burns a little fire. In the house it's warm. And the Rabbi teaches little children their ABCs..."*

He told wondrous stories of Sholem Aleichem, the Kabbalah, ghosts and goblins, never about the horrors he had seen in the war. Those he kept inside. And they tormented him daily. Some of the happiest memories I have are of a devastated, freezing landscape, horrible brushes with illness and death, and a Papa singing away the pain. He saved my life over and over again.

Memories of being put on a train, then on trucks, having socks put in my mouth so the soldiers wouldn't hear a baby's cries as we crossed the border crossings, knowing my baby brother would never make it home from the Munich hospital, hearing muffled cries all night, and sleeping next to men and women having sex in the next cot so they could prove they existed. All of that he washed away with his lullabies, all of that and the black numbers etched on the arms of his friends.

Of all the things I've been able to achieve since landing in New Orleans in 1951, the one thing I can't seem to do is return to him the gifts he gave me. He's closing in on eighty and lives in a tiny two-room apartment with newspapers in stacks three feet high from the floor and a loaded gun under his mattress. He hoards his food, his "stuff" and won't go to doctors (whom he thinks are still trying to kill him). He hangs up the phone every time one of us calls. And he refuses to open the door when any of his four children come to see him or he answers the door with a loaded 45 demanding to know what we want.

So we all stopped calling and coming by to see the Papa who seems to have abandoned his children. Because we wanted to spare him, but mostly ourselves, the pain of rejection. We send the traditional cards, often a present, the silence is devastating and the moat keeps getting wider. He makes up stories about who did what to whom and when. We hear about them from acquaintances who run into him at the grocery store. He keeps the hurts close, wrapping the stories around him like a warm blanket to keep him safe from the children who love him.

As if feelings were bullets, he needs to wear a bulletproof vest to keep him safe from the children who remind him of the ones he buried half a world away in Uzbekistan and Germany. Safe from the little girl who wanted desperately to sing away his pain - who now writes away his pain instead.

For those people who question whether the Holocaust ever happened, I am proof that there is not one, but two Holocausts that always take place. The one that slaughters human beings like cattle and with less compassion; and a second Holocaust each person who survives carries with them every day of their lives. Victims of wars they do not create. Nevertheless wake up to every day reliving those horrors, then shutting the door on love and kindness, because to risk caring is too great a hurt.

Now and then, though I rarely hear a train whistle at night these days, whenever I do the three-year-old inside me still says a little prayer, "Please dear God, don't let them come and take my Papa away."

*I wrote this Spring of 1994, after hearing an evening newscast about Holocaust deniers. It was published in a local newspaper The Link in Albuquerque, NM in 1995. My Papa died alone a few days before his 88th birthday September 2005. I read this at his funeral. Little did I know in 1994, that I was writing his eulogy.

3. WHERE DOES THE TRAIN GO, WHEN IT LEAVES MUNICH?

A tiny frightened child stands

At the bottom of a hill

Watching...

     as the train roars by through the tall pine trees

Wondering where it goes.

To someplace warm, peaceful

A place where there is space to sleep

Sunshine to warm your face?

Munich is icy cold, so full of ghosts

Corpses buried by the hands of others.

As she peeks through chocolate eyes

She wonders...

What kind of world stands silently by

      Knowingly seeing, doing nothing...

Allowing the murder of its children

While it looks the other way?

By two she's learned

Survival means silence

Old socks stuffed in mouths

Too hurt to cry out loud.

She places her needs

      Her dreams

      Her feelings aside

To be remembered

And dealt with another day.

Invisible...

She watches...

Stuffing all her screams

All the terror down too deep.

Afraid if she begins to cry

She will be unable to stop.

As a whisper...

She stands paralyzed

Watching the train moving

Through the tall pine trees.

Afraid, this time it will come and take...

...her Papa away.

4. THE FELON ACROSS THE STREET

Why is it that some grown-ups believe that hitting, spanking, beating children or animals teaches them anything at all? Children and animals learn two things from that experience. Not to trust you and to get as far away from you as possible when ever possible.

If Hazel Davis is still alive and you know her, tell her what a horrific third grade teacher she was. She must be dead for sure, unless she's 99 years old, though I doubt someone so mean would still be alive. Wishful thinking, I guess. That she was born without a heart is a given. So is the fact that she was a teacher of young children. What she taught was fear. She must have been a felon in another life; because in this life school was prison, and she was the warden.

I was a frightened tiny eight-year-old in Ms. Davis's third grade class May 1953. Fifty-six years later Aunt Judy drove me by her house last week to say goodbye to the awful memory of her. It never occurred to me to drive by alone. Her house was across the street from

our first real home in America. The mid-Phoenix neighborhood was poor, dingy, and small just a mile or so South of Osborn Road and Central Avenue. Compared to a refugee camp in Munich, it was the American Dream as created by my Father, the house painter, complete with a huge tree for climbing in the front yard. One limb extended out so far over the street, I could see the roofs of the cars as they went under me as I sat up there dangling my legs.

Judy took me for a drive around town a couple weeks back on my many visits to Phoenix. I sat in the car starring at both houses remembering not the bruised black and blue knuckles, but the embarrassment of being hit by my third grade teacher with a yardstick in front of the entire class my first day at my new school.

My parents bought their first house moving me from a tiny school of a hundred children to a gigantic monstrosity with multiple playgrounds and a thousand children at the corner of Osborn and Central. The felony that caused the beating the first day at the new school, was getting lost on a playground too far from the classroom to hear the appropriate buzzer after lunch. Different buzzers for different playgrounds, but Ms. Davis didn't care. She never even let me explain. She grabbed me, marched me up in front of her desk, took out a 12 inch wooden ruler and beat my knuckles till I cried.

For years I sat in the last seat in the last row of every class I was in. Usually the one closest to the door which would make for an easy escape. Then I met Bob Porter in eighth grade. As usual I was in the last seat in the last row. He sat in the seat in front of me. We were voting for the officers for our class. He was running for Vice-President and I was running for Treasurer. I tapped him on the shoulder and whispered, "Who are you voting for?"

He turned around and looked at me with a wrinkled forehead and question marks visible in the pupils of both eyes, "Myself, of course! If you don't think you are good enough to win, why should anyone else?"

Bob became VP of eighth grade of course. I hear he's is a black jack dealer in Vegas.

5. DON'T TRY THIS AT HOME

When you're the oldest child of immigrant parents, you plow the path as if you were in a John Deere mower. They think it's 1930 Poland or Romania depending on the week and which parent won the argument. In reality it's 1959 Phoenix, Arizona, the United States of America. They say "no" a lot, because life costs too much, they have four children to raise, and few financial resources. You have found babysitting pays. So does a savings account at the bank, which in addition pays interest.

Mostly they say "no" because they have been thrust into a life they never intended living nor in anyway feels familiar to them. Modern psychology hasn't arrived in the form of EST trainings, Ram Dass, Tony Robbins, Wayne Dyer, and weekly therapy sessions. Grateful is how you feel if you have enough money to fix the brakes on the car and buy a kosher chicken for Shabbat dinner. Grateful is in-door plumbing and a washing machine.

All your clothes are made on an old Singer; you want a cashmere sweater and matching pencil skirt and jellybeans (flat sherbet colored shoes) from Goldwater's on Central Avenue. They watch Ed Sullivan, you watch Dick Clark. You crave fitting in, they don't get it. School isn't for fitting in, school is for learning. What's wrong with you? You want to grow up and be a waitress for God's sake?

In 1959, nothing was more American than smoking. Thanks to the movies of the 1940s and 1950s, everybody who was anybody smoked; and I wanted to be everybody. I wanted to be cool. If you were cool, you were leaning against the wall in the halls of Central High wearing a pale green or pink cashmere pencil skirt (very tight) and the same color sweater (even tighter). Babysitting earnings did not pay for cashmere. Besides, I couldn't inhale and I never looked or acted weak in public. Remember last row near the door, speedy exit Sara. People made fun of you if you weren't cool or tough.

In my dreams, I'm leaning against the wall with my right leg bent at the knee, the bottom of my green jellybeans against the same wall. James Dean is handing me a drag off his cigarette that has recently touched his lips, just before he reaches down and touches mine. All the really popular girls are walking by whispering, "How did she land him? What happened to Julie Harris?"

In my dreams. Wide a wake, I remember there's a tiny problem. James Dean died five years earlier and I can't inhale without gagging, coughing, and seeming a complete inept moron. Who's going to kiss that? No problem – *my mind has a mind of it's own*. Not sure if I made it up or borrowed it, but it accurately describes my brain.

Quick trip to the bank and the grocery store (walking, I'm only 14). *Kents*, I heard of those. Oh no, where to hide them so Mom's angel doesn't find out and tattle on me. *Marjorie Morningstar*, my latest read by Herman Wouk. (So you know, I don't read books, I devour them. When I find a book I love, I find every book that author has ever written and devour those as well. Number of pages doesn't matter.) Put the pack of cigarettes between the back cover and the last page. Flat cigarettes, no problem, they'll light up. But where? Where can I commit this felony without getting caught and sent to Florence Prison?

I know, the Steinberg's house Saturday night. Great! Saturday night arrives and the children have an 8 pm bedtime. It's 9 pm, I read them a story, now they're fast asleep down the hall of the long hallway ranch home with their door closed.

For those of you who don't know, summer in Phoenix is stifling. Crank up the cooler and open the sliding glass door all the way so the air gets pushed out instead of recycled. Find large bowl type glass ashtray that's washable.

Directions for committing felony: Sit down on the couch; get matches, set ashtray down, light up cigarette one. Cough, spit, gurgle, then try to breathe, light up cigarette two. Proceed to the end of the pack taking two hours to acquire this new habit creating a sexy hot chick.

Results of committing felony: Oh my God! Who's bright idea was this? That stupid angel, must have been his. I'm dying, never mind I'm green. Too bad I don't have the cashmere outfit, I'd match. Flush everything down the toilet after chopping up the package, wash the ashtray, the sink, all the while I'm holding my rib cage with my right arm, figuring this is my last day on earth so I better make sure the kitchen and family room are spotless. Ashes anywhere, nope. The Steinbergs arrive home, hand me money, and say in astonishment, "Sara, you don't look so good, do you want a ride home?"

Well duh...she responds, "I'm fine, I'll walk. (It's still 100 degrees outside.) I think maybe I have a cold. My throat hurts."

Two blocks home, fall into bed; sleep like a dead person, never waking up in the morning, Mom will come in and find my cold body. What is that light, it can't be morning yet. Drag myself up and into the kitchen for juice.

Nusha takes one look smell, "What is wrong with you? You look terrible."

"My throat hurts, I think I have a cold," says lying Sara.

"In July? You've been smoking!" she responds incredulously.

"Me smoke, never!" says the eldest daughter.

6. REDHEAD WITH A VIEW

Can you believe it? Hitler didn't kill all the Jews in Europe during the Second World War. He left our family a couple of cousins still alive in Pittsburgh. The truth being they left Europe before the war started. Uncle Aron found them – real live cousins in Pittsburgh. "Fageh" (Fae) is coming for a visit in July by plane. Oh the excitement, the joy, the baking, the trip to Sky Harbor Airport at two in the afternoon with six people in an emerald green Lincoln with a white leather top and white leather seats to match. It's about 122 degrees in the car and out on the tarmac in Phoenix in the summer.

Sky Harbor is a very small airport with one terminal, no freeway entrances, just a couple of signs with arrows. We are all waiting with faces peering through the chain-link fence, waiting for Fae Talisman (our only real live

37

relative in America) to come down the stairs of the little plane that just landed on the scorching tarmac. The door opens, the stairs come down and people begin deplaning. Mom yells "Fagehnu" and starts jumping up and down and waving. There she is!

Oh my God, there's Marilyn Monroe coming to take a vacation at our house in Phoenix descending the stairs. This version has Irish red flowing hair and a strapless white dress with flowers, her beautiful feet have on wooden 5" stilettos with red toenails, and her hands have 2" red fingernails that scratch.

I can't breathe, I can't speak, I'm envisioning DNA molecules, (like those Norbert Konzal, my Biology teacher, showed us in class at Central High), twirling faster and faster in my brain. Oh my God, we're related. I'm almost fifteen now, but wait till I'm eighteen; I'm definitely going to be a knockout. I just need a few props. And Fae has props. She is gorgeous. She is a cougar for sure! They didn't have cougars or babes back then though as Simon Cowell so frequently says, "I don't know what 'it' is but I know it when I see it."

You don't need many props when you're gorgeous with red flowing hair, wearing a red and pink flowered strapless dress with a full skirt and ruching in back. I can tell she really likes me. I am totally enamored and in desperate need of an older female ally. Nun Nusha (my Mother) thinks I am still six years old and wants to keep me a baby forever. She won't even let me wear a dress to synagogue unless I wear a girdle and nylons. And flat shoes, I have to wear flat shoes. A curse if you're only 5' tall. I desperately need 5" black patent leather stilettos. I could never go to college without them. Enter Faye AKA Marilyn, savior, and my new BFF (best friend forever).

We get in our green and white Lincoln with white leather seats, burn our respective tushes and drive home. You haven't lived until you've experienced getting into a car with leather seats that has been sitting out in the sun in a Phoenix parking lot during the summer. Might be why they wore girdles and hose when it was 122 outside.

Fae is staying in my room since I'm the only one with the extra bed and a girl (besides did I mention she's my BFF). We put her suitcase on the extra bed and I sit on my twin bed observing this gorgeous creature (obviously soon to be discovered by a Hollywood mogul and stolen from me for sure). I'm inhaling the view as most 14-year-old high school girls would that are being raised by a Jewish Nun – my mother Bubbie Nusha (also known as the other Faye).

It's hotter than hell even with the swamp cooler at full blast. Fae opens her suitcase for a change of clothes. She pulls out a pair of white shorts and a pink halter-top that ties around the neck and in back and lays them on the bed. In one motion she grabs the ruching on both sides of the floral dress and yanks down.

My forty something second cousin (the same age as my Mother the Nun) is commando. No bra, no panties, no slip, nothing at all. Full frontal nothing on under that dress! The only thing she is wearing are the stilettos and a pair of huge hoop earrings. My brain instantly becomes Jell-O. The same color as my face. All I can think of is that she came across the United States in a plane with nothing on underneath in 5" wooden stilettos with red hot painted toenails.

"DNA doesn't lie," says Mr. Konzal. I'm going to be stunning, I'm going to go naked under my clothes, I'm going to stop traffic, and then fly across the country in a plane with nothing on underneath my dress. And I'm going to be a redhead. Just as soon as I get out of college, get a job, get a car, get an apartment, and live very far away from my Mother the Nun, also known as Bubbie Nusha.

7. THE GIRLS REALLY LIKE THIS

Every time Aron called Phoenix from Detroit, he would share stories of his wealth, friends, and apartment on Nine Mile Road. Aronchik (Mom's youngest sibling) eventually became a successful entrepreneur, though summer of 1964 he was still trying to figure out how to get his electrical contractor's license, tell his ex-wife they were divorced six months earlier, and date women with a 14 year old nephew and a 18 year old niece staying with him in a 500 sq ft one bedroom apartment that had an accordion door separating the 3 foot kitchen from the rest of the place.

There are a few baby boomers' coming of age fantasies that involve Patrick Swazye and a dance floor. I'm not that fortunate. My coming of age memories are a trip to Detroit, a pole lamp with colored lights (no dancing girls), and a grown up party with blonds sitting on green couch arms with their long legs crossed at the ankle wearing pencil skirts and tight sweaters in pastel colors. One tall blond whispering to me, "We knew there was a woman staying here. There are napkins on the table."

Aronchik at thirty-three included girls, friends, girls, food, girls, fun, girls – the daily agenda. Though the major priority was the acquisition of money. Lots of cash which one carried in bags in the trunk of one's car. Never knew when you might need a few coins for the meter or bialys and whitefish at the deli. It's a simple algebraic equation $(A + M = W)$. Aron plus lots of money equaled women. Back then, when men actually paid for dinner and a date was dinner and dancing, but I digress. You needed lots of cash to dress the part, drive the car, and get the girl. And Aron played the part with gusto.

It took me all freshman year to save up for the ticket to Detroit. An eighteen year old female traveling alone by train from Phoenix to Detroit during the days when no matter how hot it got, a dignified female wore a girdle, nylons, a black pleated skirt, sweater, and high heeled pumps. Even with all those undergarments, it was liberating being alone at last with strangers in the big world.

For seventy-two hours I was an adult on my own in a safe place – the Silver Streak bound for Detroit. Hitchcock might have had a different of view of trains, but my Mother was in Phoenix and it was way before cell phones, texting, and computers. Free at last, free at last, no Mother, riding the rails through Kansas on my way to Detroit, I was free at last. Pure unadulterated freedom staring back at me through the window at seventy-five miles per hour. All dressed up where to go? The dining car with white tablecloths, white linen napkins, white china cups with saucers – for drinking coffee with seven teaspoons of sugar and real cream.

Like any number of my storybook heroines, I was on my way to the big city to see my very handsome Uncle, stay at his bachelor pad, and sleep on his emerald green Danish couch with teak legs. Normal people live in Detroit and vacation in Phoenix during the winter. Then there's me.

Three days later, after a train change in Chicago, Aron picks me up at the train station. As we are entering the narrow hallway of the bachelor pad on Nine Mile Road, Aron is behind me telling me to turn on the light switch in the early afternoon. So I flip the specially installed light switch to one of those 1960s teak pole lamps with five lights in red, blue, yellow, and green at intervals all the way to the ceiling. Lights flashing at odd intervals. This pole is changing colors like the neon lights in those police dramas on prime time television. I turn and look at Aronchik incredulous. He smiles like a little boy checking out a new bicycle at Christmas. "I installed it myself," says Aron behind me with a smile and a wink. "The girls really like this."

8. HIAWATHA WATAHAMAGEE

November 1968, eleven months after we were married, my husband (the pharmacist working for the Public Health Service in Parker, AZ so he doesn't have to go to Vietnam), decides that it would be an adventure to check out the drug cabinet at the base of the Grand Canyon; where the Havasupai Indians live on a reservation of several hundred people next to the Colorado River. Philip loved adventures.

"Ever been on a horse," asks Hubby?

"Oh sure, lot's of times," I respond. (Once when I was twelve but who's counting.)

It's November 1st, we wake at 2 a.m., drive for two hours mostly over rocks to get to a dirt road, with even more rocks to arrive at a hilltop in Peach Springs (not far from Kingman). Violá we are somewhere on a knoll at the top of the canyon in the dark. Its minus five degrees. I'm wearing several layers of clothing, including a red wool car coat with a hood and gloves. There is no getting warm. The only place to pee is one of those blue portable potty places. It's so cold that inside the outhouse you can hear the wind whistle. There's a Havasupai guide waiting for us holding the reins of three large horses.

"Ever ridden before," asks Hiawatha Watahamagee our guide? (I swear I'm not making this up.)

"Oh sure, I ride all the time," says the 23 year old idiot with oatmeal for brains. Moron is actually a much better word, but I digress.

The horse steps off the cliff's edge and we are on a dirt trail that is probably less that 30 inches wide with a 3000 foot drop straight down on my left with no railing. I am either too young or too stupid to realize how grave the danger. Hiawatha is in front of me and Philip in back. If I fall it will likely be sideways.

Three hours later we finally arrive at the bottom of the switchback trail at the base of the canyon. My very independent horse decides he knows a short cut to his stable. Trigger is in a huge hurry to get home. He takes off at full gallop with me lying on top fiercely grasping his mane, the horn of the saddle, and anything else I could cling to for dear life. We are on the shores of the Colorado River and there are boulders the size of a Volkswagen bug everywhere I look, which is easy from my angle of lying on top of the horse with the reins in my hands, my feet desperately trying to stay in the stirrups, in my Little Red Riding Hood jacket blowing behind me, hearing my hubby screaming "Sara hold on!"

Yup, that's me the experienced horse woman. I'm going to do one of them Lone Ranger jump from one side to the other tricks at forty-five miles an hour with rocks on either side. An eternity later we arrive at the ranch and Trigger stops to get a drink. I don't have a scratch on me anywhere.

That's when you hear the angel on your right shoulder holding on to the hair on the back of your neck, shaking his head, "Wait till God hears about this! Moron, did I bring you from Tashkent to the bottom of the Grand Canyon so you could kill yourself?" Hey, what do you want? My angel has an attitude and sounds like my Mother.

Other people's children merely shave their heads, get a tattoo, or dye their hair a ridiculous color of orange or purple. Then there's me. I can be talked into almost anything by almost anyone. At least once, if they come bringing chocolate truffles.

My son once asked in high school how come I let him make so many of his own mistakes and didn't intervene the way most of his friends' Mothers did. Hopefully this story many years later answers that question. When you do stuff in your youth that would scare your Mother to death if she knew, you have to give your children the gift of learning lessons they need to learn on their own as well.

9. GOD IS NOT A WOMAN

It was my second year of law school and life was exciting. The woman that was too afraid to speak till I was sixteen (as my Mother once shared with my upstairs neighbor Rick) now got on her soap box about everything female and everything unjust. Which was just about everything that existed, particularly men. The year was 1975, and God was woman! Hear her roar. Just ask Gloria Steinem, Bella Abzug, and Betty Friedan.

My mouth was bigger than I was. Outside I was tiny, thin, feisty, smart, confident, and boisterous. Inside I was huge, lonely, and had a hole the size of the Grand Canyon growing next to my heart. Growing exponentially larger daily. Denial can be as dangerous to one's soul as an undetected tumor is to one's body. Though that's for another day and another lifetime. Books were my refuge and Black's Law Dictionary the biggest book I could find. If it was in print, in black and white, it must be accurate, it must be true, it must be authentic. Have you never read The Old Testament?

We had so many women's lib discussions, my friends and I. It was as if the Women's Liberation Movement gave women a chance to exhale for the first time in a thousand years. There is always someone who doesn't believe in God; though for most of us, who do believe, we were positive she was female. Finally, after a millennium our time had come. Our voices would be heard and even listened to by the disbelievers. We would surely be heard and acknowledged. She would show us a sign.

All my friends, except one – Robin Miller. Robin used to say, not only was she positive that God was not a female, she was certain to her core that God was a man. When I asked her once why she was so sure that God was not female, the neo-natal nurse who had worked the night shift in the emergency room at Long Beach Memorial for more than twenty years laughed out loud and said, "If God were a woman we'd all have been born with zippers."

10. MILITARY-INDUSTRIAL-COMPLEX

My brother Moishe wondered out loud a lot and wasn't shy about letting anyone know how he felt about anything. He told the entire family that I had sold out to the military-industrial complex. Law school had ended, I hadn't passed the California Bar, the divorce was final, and we were living on $200 a month, with rent at $180 plus what I could earn clerking at Pomona Superior Court and whatever law office needed a temp that week. Don't ask me how I raised a son by myself; with virtually no financial assistance from his Father, I wondered about that enough every time I checked the final settlement agreement. Wondered about that every time I bought groceries, but I wanted the divorce. Adulthood hit me in the face like an 18-wheeler that doesn't stop.

I was always really good at earning lots of money. I just didn't believe that I deserved to keep it for very long. General Dynamics offered me a $16,000 annual salary with vacation pay and health insurance. It's what we desperately needed.

June of 1978, I thought I had won the lottery. My friends were making less than $7,000 as starting teachers. It may not have offered me the opportunity to be a litigator in a courtroom like my idol Perry Mason, but it was solid work and paid well. The light was shinning at the end of my tunnel and I didn't need glasses to see it. I started my career negotiating contracts and never looked back. I was making double what most of my law school classmates who were clerking for $4.00 to $7.00 an hour with no benefits were making and I had an expense account.

In 1978, professional women with credentials under 35 were just getting started. With Helen Reddy's *I Am Woman* playing in my head, I went on the interview of my life – it lasted more than three hours. My resume was heavy on the education, light on work experience. At the end of three hours, when asked why I didn't have more experience, frustrated and exasperated I blurted out "How do I get experience when no one will hire me."

I have found that most times the truth isn't anything most people want to hear, though in this case I started four days later as Jack Peterson's new Contract Administrator. Seems that General Dynamics was under a Federal injunction to hire women and my resume said Juris Doctorate.

Men and I have always had strained relationships, except when it came to work. And though I didn't pay attention to life's details back then like I do now, God was sending me a test. A really big test. I love men, they love me, then the deserving part kicks in, and I find a reason to bale. General Dynamics was a huge test with a capital H. When you really don't believe you deserve something, you may receive it from the universe, but you will always manage to find a way to screw it up after all is said and done.

So its Monday, first day on the job. I come to work early all dressed in my new business suit – white slinky blouse with bow tie in front, black pencil skirt (tight, nothing has changed in the eighteen years since high school), black hose, and black stilettos (4" patent leather, Carrie would be proud). Drug screening, paperwork, secret clearance paperwork, details, details and even more details this was a Department of Defense (DOD) facility. I am walked to Jack Peterson's office we chat and I laugh appropriately at the right times, and have the blushing at the right time down on queue. I'm a girl aren't I? He takes me from his office to my desk in the Contract Administration bullpen, a room the size of half a Home Depot. There are three rows of Navy desks, all dark gray and newly repainted. My desk is in the center of the room. "Thank you, Mr. Peterson." I sit down to start my new job and pick up the phone to call my first customer and look up.

Men - I am in a sea of men and I know how to swim. Men in the right row, men in the left row, and men in my row with me in the middle – every color, every race, every size. Except for the secretary, I am the only female in a room the size of a grocery store. Oh my

God, what am I going to do? Punt Sara, my brain always kicks in first. Smile Sara smile, blush Sara blush, drool Sara drool...

Oh my God, what am I wearing to work tomorrow?

11. INGENUOUS CENTERFOLD

Ted Cohen, a friend's husband, once looked at me over Thanksgiving dinner as I was telling yet another story and said, "Jeez, Sara you are so ingenuous!" I remember Ted sitting across the table shaking his head with a smile on his face and a look. Still not sure what that was all about, but I remember grabbing the Webster's when I got home (no Dictionary.com in the 1980's). Me – *naïve, innocent, frank, guileless,* - not possible. Why would he say that? I am not naïve. Never was, never will be. I'm smart, I have street sense. You could drop me off anywhere in the world and I'd find my way home. And the rest of it is nonsense. A woman needs to be smart, talk well, and smile. It's called the "female card" which I knew how to play on automatic pilot.

Then my mind, with a mind of its own, generally takes over and says, "...but what about General Dynamics?" Its 1979, I've been at the military-industrial-complex in Pomona about seven months. Seven months of getting up every morning at 4:30 am checking to see what new dress or skirt I'm going to wear to impress this man or that guy. Used to wear pants since I fell in love with Katherine Hepburn and jeans in the late 50's; however, when you're surrounded by fifty men daily, you don't wear pants. You wear a black pencil skirt (short but not too short, have to be able to bend over without looking like a slut), black hose, and stilettos. And, if you can find a pair of black patent stilettos with a shiny aluminum metal stripe starting at the top of the back of the shoe going all the way down to the bottom of the heel, well watch out Carrie Bradshaw.

Jack Peterson is now the Director of the Contracts Department and once a week on Fridays in lieu of our lunch hour, we all lunch together with sandwiches delivered from the local deli, to discuss the status of the week's contracts. Me in a conference room with fifty men; "Dear Lord thank you! What wonderful thing did I do in my last life to deserve such good fortune?" I'm sitting in a conference room upholstered chair with casters on the legs. Which, thank God, push all the way under the gigantic table so no one will know that my stiletto clad feet miss the floor by three inches.

While we are nibbling on sandwiches, before we get to the statistics of the week, one of the guys decides to start a conference room table game called - *When you were in high school, what did you want to be when you became an adult?* What is wrong with men anyway?

Off we go around the table, with each story funnier than the next - the usual fireman, policeman, F-16 pilot, accountant, Marine Corp sergeant, inventor, surfer dude, rock star, and on and on. The stories are getting closer to my side of the gigantic walnut table; I have to think fast (not a good situation for me to be in as no one had informed me yet, that I was ingenuous). Lights, action, camera, quiet on the set, and the actress speaks her lines, "I always wanted to be a Playboy bunny centerfold." I don't understand, why this is so funny. Why is everyone laughing hysterically? Why am I turning red? Why is Mr. Peterson shaking his head at me again? Did I spill my lunch on my white sweater?

Remember when Aunt Judy told you, "Better to keep your mouth shut and be thought a fool, then to open it and remove all doubt." Remember that line Sara? Where have you been since seventh grade? It gets better, because sitting to my left is the adorable Contracts Department clown Dante Fierros who hasn't had a turn yet. "Dante," Mr. Peterson says hoping the laughter dies down soon so we can end this nonsense and get on to business. Dante looks to his right - me head down, still bright red to my stiletto toes, "I always wanted to be a Playboy bunny photographer."

Mr. Peterson still shaking his head leaves the conference room and tells us to go back to our desks when we have finished lunch. I think the Vice President of Contracts called him later to find out why we were having so much fun.

12. SIGNIFICANCE

September 1979, during my first week at Airesearch in Torrance, CA my new boss Brent asked me about the ACES II F-16 ejection seat contracts I was administering. I looked back at him with blank eyes. "What product are you selling? How does it work? Have you seen it or touched it? What's a class C explosive," Mr. Green wanted to know standing at the entrance to my tiny gray cubicle? I looked at him in total disbelief. I was a Contract Manager. I knew about the law, finance, protecting the company's interests. My degree was in law, I wasn't an Engineer. I was a conscientious employee, experienced, committed, came with references, came to work on time. Why did I need to know how an ejection seat worked? I knew what a contract was. I had been in school forever and spent a fortune learning those principles and he was doubting my smarts. Discrimination based on sex that's what this was. What difference could it possibly make that the seat was *man-rated*?

"No," I responded, "I don't."

"Come with me," Brent said.

Off we went for a three-hour tour of the company. I met Gary, the Buyer, who purchased parts that went into the seat; I met John the Manufacturing Manager, Sheldon the Test Engineer, Clifton the Engineering Program Manager, his boss Sumner, and Evelyn, the woman on the manufacturing line who installed the wires on the printed circuit boards. I viewed the clean room where the sensors (that flew the seats) were made, looked through a microscope while a man installed gold wires so small they needed tweezers to hold them while soldering, and learned that our company (the only one in the world) owned all the patents for this process.

Ours was the only company that was authorized to produce these sensors for the United States Air Force. I could feel myself becoming proud of landing this unbelievable job. I found myself becoming more intelligent following, listening, and of course smiling (a lot). I found respect on a manufacturing line, and dignity in a shipping department. Astonishing myself most, that none of it came from the law degree still in the box in the garage because I had managed to flunk the California Bar Exam not once but twice (on purpose). I guess I really didn't want to be an attorney after all. Sorry Perry.

Surely this was some kind of cosmic joke. Maybe, though before the day ended, I even knew the names of guys in the shipping department who made sure our seats were packed in such a way that they didn't eject during transport.

Later that day I asked my boss if this was a necessary part of my employment? "Absolutely," said Mr. Green. "In your career you will meet many people. All are significant. They deserve your attention and care, even if all you do is smile and say "hello." You will be asked to sell or negotiate products you know nothing about. How can you possibly handle yourself in an intelligent, confident manner if you have no knowledge of these products?"

I never forgot the lesson of significance. During my seven years there, I also met the President and Vice-President of Airesearch. They came to visit me often, stopping to say "hi" to the Contract Manager who smiled a lot and regularly went to visit the people on the manufacturing line; as well as bringing boxes of jelly donuts to the guys out in shipping Christmas week.

One October they came to ask me how much of a discount I had given one of our customers warranting the incredible 3 foot tall sunflower chrysanthemum floral arrangement that was sitting on my desk? That I had received from Ron Guse for my birthday.

Many years after I left the company my last boss there, Glenn Earl called and told me that Brent had called him and told him he never should have let me leave. He had to hire three administrators to replace me after I was gone.

13. FOOTPRINTS ON MY HEART

The best girlfriend I ever had was a buyer named Ron. Ron was my dear friend, my soul mate for about 10 years. He was gay, I wasn't. I sold ejection seat sensors for the F-16 ACES II ejection seats. Ron was the buyer for the company that made those seats. He got me a yellow "eject" handle from the F-16 scrap bin for my RX-7. I used it to threaten my son's teenage friends with a trip through the moon roof. They all thought I was "real cool."

I loved him so much I threw a birthday party for him January 1983. He showed up in chaps. Thank God he was wearing jeans underneath. My friend Joey asked him if he was cold. He laughed. When I went to his house we would go shopping for material for curtains, which he would then sew, calling me to ask what colors went with what.

He was 6' 4", blond, stunningly gorgeous, had abs no one would believe, and came to my office wearing beige slacks (with a pressed fold), a hot pink golf shirt, a white jacket, loafers no socks. I'm 4' 11" and everyone in the building thought he was madly in love with me and we were having an affair. One could dream. He exaggerated everything to the hilt, driving his aqua Cadillac convertible with white leather seats down Hollywood Blvd. He called me "Babe" and "Dear" during a time when everyone minded, but me.

Everyday, he called screaming at 9 a.m. and 1 p.m. sharp. I would lay the phone on my desk speaker side up and let him scream for 30 minutes. The secretary and I would look at each other and howl silently. We were always late on parts. He would drive down from Glendale to Torrance and scream at all the big wig vice presidents. My boss would hand me $400 in cash and tell me to get him out of building. "Take him to lunch, anywhere he wants to go," came the edict from Glenn.

We would leave in my RX-7, go to Redondo Beach, and wait till we crossed 190th Street to start laughing. Lunch was three hours of gossip and stories – mostly whom he picked up on Hollywood Blvd in the aqua Caddy. It was 1982 and the aids virus was only a whisper in certain circles. What did I know? I didn't travel in those circles.

If I could have one redo of a year it would be 1992. It was not a good year for me on any level – personally or professionally. He died that spring of complications from the aids virus. I remember so many tiny details of the ten years we were best friends I often surprise myself.

After the funeral I sent his Mother a card that read "Some people come into our lives and quickly go, some stay for a while, leaving footprints on our hearts, and we are never ever the same."

14. SHADES OF BLUE

For me, remembering shades of blue is learning to speak the truth, as well as writing in a universal language. As I often felt my single biggest problem has been – being misunderstood. I get furious because I assume that other people know what I mean when I say something and they don't. Then I conjure up they are intentionally giving me a hard time because it's much more enjoyable to be difficult than to attempt to understand what I'm saying. In other words, they're giving me a hard time on purpose.

Heaven forbid that I might be communicating in a manner that is frustrating to them or they really do not know what I mean. Or that I'm doing my usual going in eighteen verbal directions at once, always knowing where I am, but seeing in their eyes that they are lost. How can my family members not know, when I'm perfectly clear and intelligent? Huh? After all they've known me forever, right?

It's Saturday morning in Long Beach where you can find me painting yet another wall in my dining room of the 1932 California bungalow home I love with the red oak floors and fifty year old rose bushes. I'm a nester and have been since I became an adult. All those early childhood years in a refugee camp took there toll on me. Having a special home to live in is about the most important thing on earth to me.

I love painting, arranging, decorating, and have only recently given up hanging wallpaper. Mostly because I could have taken an African Safari or a trip to Paris for what I spent in the Laura Ashley store at South Coast Plaza for twelve years.

It's the mid-eighties and once again I am revising the color of the dining room. What with Josh's Bar Mitzvah taking place at the end of summer, the dining room with wanes coating dividing every wall that used to be duck egg blue with two tone striped wallpaper, will become the hot new style Country French in Wedgwood blue. Everybody is coming to the Bar Mitzvah and I want to show off my beautiful house, changing my mind yet again from two tone stripes to two toned flowers.

Personally (and I know this to be a fact), I was the profit margin for Laura Ashley, Ralph Lauren, and Home Depot. Their stock dropped considerably when I left Los Angeles in 1992. Saturdays were spent painting and Sunday mornings were spent at Home Depot finding a new project for the following week. If not for me these stores would have gone bankrupt for sure. Look at that,

I'm helping the American economy all by myself. I am a heroine. An exhausted one as I work full time driving an hour each way to and from work on the Los Angeles freeways, but a heroine nevertheless.

"What are you doing?" the voice asks as I pick up the receiver Saturday morning.

"Hi Moishe, I'm painting the dining room."

"Again," my brother says incredulous. "What color are you painting it this time?"

"Wedgwood," I respond.

"What? What the hell color is that?" questions Moishe getting ready to be miffed.

"You know, Wedgwood. The color of the plates."

"What plates?" asks Moishe.

"Wedgwood plates, the ones made in England."

"Well what color is that?" says Moishe. Seriously beginning to lose his patience with my obviously moronic behavior. Obvious to everyone but me.

"Well, it's a kind of blue-ish gray. I don't know exactly how to describe it. You know Wedgwood," shocked that he does not fathom what I mean.

By this point the brother who called to ask me to breakfast would like to put his hands around my throat and squeeze. We do a little more *"who's on first"* and finally I say, "It's a shade of blue!"

"Why didn't you say so at the beginning?" says Moishe, by now shouting.

"Because there are 5000 shades of blue," say I even louder.

"You're breaking my ear drum! Why are you always screaming at me?" says Moishe.

And there's the rub, the dichotomy, the yo-yo. We're smart, we're clear. We understand how these 26 letters combine and twist and turn and what they mean. Why we've been using them our entire lives. We certainly know what we mean! Don't we? How can the person standing next to or in front of or on the phone not get it?

We even spend thousands of dollars, time and effort going to therapists whining about how we've been wronged using even more words, with more meanings. We get divorced over who left the cap off the toothpaste. Yes you did! No I didn't!

So the conversation continues for at least thirty minutes with each of us batting the verbal badminton back and forth across the airwaves for one to whack back to the other, with each return louder than the other. All that wasted energy, lost emotional revenue, and time arguing about shades of blue when we could have been having eggs benedict.

15. YOU MEET NO STRANGERS

Edith, her cousin Nancy (both well over seventy), and I met on an America West flight back to Los Angeles from San Antonio May 1991. I noticed Edith while I was waiting in the airport for the flight that would take me back to Long Beach (where I lived) after negotiating a contract at San Antonio Air Force Base. She was dressed head to toe in black with a black hat and special black glasses wrapping the top half of her face indicating she had a problem with her eyesight. The only colored clothing was a noticeable neon lime green jacket covered with huge red and yellow roses. It was like meeting Spring. She must be an artist, I thought. As it turned out, we were sitting next to each other when the plane took off and I had guessed correctly.

My career as a poet was two months old; I was handwriting all my poems in a tiny spiral notebook, which I carried with me everywhere. God forbid I should miss a letter or a thought. I was writing feverishly in the aisle seat while we were taking off, and they both noticed. Hadn't even reached the novice stage yet. We started talking, I shared my notebook of poems, and Nancy gave me their calling cards in white lace gloved hands. When I arrived home, I wrote *Beautiful Ladies* and mailed it to San Antonio, Texas to the seventy year old cousins. Turns out Edith Kroshel was a renowned watercolor artist who had been commissioned by the City of San Antonio to paint the Alamo.

She sent me a thank you letter with a note, *"Thank you for seeing past the wrinkles."* Hand written on pale blue tissue paper. Edith and I have been corresponding since that airplane ride. She now lives in a retirement home in Texas and sends me letters written with a magnifying glass and tiny drawings of her surroundings. I respond in 18 pt font so she can see the words. Recently she wrote that she's been reading my poems to her exercise swim class. While the "girls" are doing kicks in the pool, Edith is reading my love poems out loud. Imagine that!

Guess when you share your gifts of gratitude; you never really know how far your gifts will travel. In retrospect, I guess one should always return more cookies to the cookie jar than one takes out. Then the cookie jar is always full, and so is your heart!

16. BEAUTIFUL LADIES

Beautiful Ladies

Some ladies
     in black hats, and
         red flowered
Green jackets,
     have a way of entering a place,
        making heads turn,
           no matter their age.
Society teaches us
     to be envious of

beautiful young women,
with tight bodies,
forced smiles, and
unfulfilled vacant eyes...

Having been twenty, thirty,
even forty and fifty...
Sometimes looking at life
Through a rearview mirror...
I'm sure, given the chance,
I'm looking forward
to becoming
a beautiful lady...
...in a black hat and
red flowered green jacket.

17. A VIRGIN & A PAUPER

In 1991, my newly discovered writing talent scared the hell out of me. I kept it a secret from everyone I knew. I was a contract administrator. I handled important government documents. I had a DOD Secret Clearance for God's sake. I sold F-16 seats for a living! I worked for the military-industrial-complex. I did NOT (are you listening God) write poetry. As much as I loved Emily Dickinson, E.E. Cummings, and James Kavanaugh, who did I think I was? A poet? A writer? Me? Surely you jest and I have magically appeared in an alternate universe.

What if they found out that late at night at home on my new Mac, I was writing love poems of loss and longing, hunger and sex. In free verse that didn't rhyme, no less. Oh my God, the humiliation, the embarrassment, the giggles. High school all over again. I might even get fired. Contract Administrators, forty-six year old left brain mothers do not suddenly awake one day espousing free verse about feelings and emotions, wanting to do nothing else except write. Whom was I kidding? If I didn't stop this falderal immediately, the poetry police would show up and lock down my Mac. I definitely needed therapy or at least to leave Los Angeles. And quickly. Where was a Bekins truck when you needed one? Uncle Aron said Los Angeles was a terrible place to live. There had to be a PA (Poets Anonymous) meeting somewhere in Los Angeles? There were meetings for every addiction known to mankind with acronyms to match. Where were the yellow pages when you needed them?

Josh was in his junior year of college taking screenplay writing classes with every certainty he would write the next great screenplay. He wouldn't leave home. Why should he? I paid for his lifestyle and let him borrow the RX-7 when he had a date or totaled the latest car he was driving that month. All his friends had a place to hang out during earthquakes; and should a tsunami follow, the fridge was always full of food so all his buddies could camp at our house. We lived five miles east of the Pacific Ocean, food was free, I did all the cooking, paid all the bills, and knocked on the door before entering his room. If God hadn't intervened I'd still be working eighteen hour days, living with him and whatever girlfriend wanted to come over and play during daylight hours when Mom was at work. As usual I digress, sorry. So many stories, so little time.

I would sit down after work, pull out my tiny spiral chamois notebook (that Mead went everywhere with me), along with my Uniball blue 10 pt fine pens, I purchased by the box. I'd be typing oblivious to time or hour, when I would feel him behind me reading over my right shoulder. He would want me to read the poem aloud. Then came the question, "How long did that take you?" For him it was always pragmatic, about mathematics not feelings. His mathematical brain working the next angle. One day instead of the math comment out comes, "Mom, you do realize that Emily Dickinson died a virgin and a pauper?"

To which I retorted, "Well I have her beat on one count. I've had sex once in my life." He left the room. His dream of inheriting a trust fund wasn't coming to fruition quickly enough. After writing from March to August 1991, I needed a large three-ring binder with alphabetic tabs.

One Sunday in August, Josh knowing my fear of speaking in front of crowds, drags me to Portofino's - a college hang out near California State University, Long Beach. Sunday nights they had the latest local rock group perform with poetry readings during intermission.

Terrified does not properly convey my state of fear. My son, the soon to be Academy Award winning playwright, who was majoring in "writing screenplays" at Steven Spielberg's stomping ground, wanted me (his mother) to come read my poems to his friends. His sneaky brain at work, I will be dead by Monday morning from heart failure; and he will inherit the house, the jazz CDs, and the RX-7. Not to worry. Now he can have women over any time he wants, not just while I'm at work.

Off we go, me hugging the 3-inch white three-ring binder with "Poetry" written in black magic marker on the side. So tight there are nail marks in the vinyl still.

We sit in back listening to the band while I can only hearing my heartbeat, waiting for intermission.

My powers of observation are excellent even when I'm terrified. There are roughly 99 people in attendance, 77 college females, a few males, band members, and staff. I'm shaking. Intermission arrives I'm the last poet to read and the only one in the room over 20. I read poem one (not bad a little clapping), didn't throw up. I read poem two, a little more noise from the girls (guess angst is appreciated amongst female intellectuals or so Moishe claims) - I *SNAP*.

Guess the applause went to my head. I turn the alphabet dividers to *"O."* I read *Orgasms and Other Feelings.** The room explodes with 77 college girls are on there feet cheering at the top of their lungs. Noise that could be heard at the Marriott on Ocean Boulevard a couple of miles away.

Note to college boys / men – never ever give your Mother a hard time about anything. Not if she can write or speak. A time will come when she remembers.

18. ORGASMS & OTHER FEELINGS

We learned early on

Not to talk about "them..."

Orgasms...

    ...and other feelings.

So women grew up wondering

What one was

Feeling cheated

If they didn't have multiple ones

As read about in Cosmo...

We didn't know much

Though we were sure

Men must be the culprits

And held them responsible.

We traded in our mates

Our husbands

Exchanging partners

Looking for the "them"

And divorce became the right of passage

To adulthood.

Whose to blame? Who knows?

If the truth be told

No one can teach you to be unafraid

You need to learn it...

       ...for yourself

19. YIDDISH "F" WORDS

"Yiddish doesn't have cuss words," Danny Thomas informed us on the Ed Sullivan Show when I was nine. It was my first language along with German spoken in the refugee camp. My father spoke Polish and Yiddish, my mother spoke Romania and Yiddish (and five other languages). I remember sitting in front of the large light wood cabinet holding the television on Sunday nights. Ed Sullivan did his "Ladies and Gentleman... Danny Thomas" who came on stage doing stand-up comedy. Funny Jewish jokes being told by a Lebanese American. He understood what it meant to be an immigrant in a new land. My kind of guy.

He said that Yiddish didn't have any dirty words, like "F" words. So if you wanted to cuss someone out in Yiddish you should say the following: "dee zolst vaksin vee a

tzsibaleh mit dem kop in draert and deh fees aroff."
Loosely translated: "you should grow like an onion with
your head in the ground and your feet in the air." The
audience would roar with laughter.

I would get so excited I couldn't sleep on Sunday night.
A world renowned man spoke Yiddish on television. On
the Ed Sullivan Show, where important came to sing,
dance, and talk. I wasn't strange because I was an
immigrant; I could grow up and become someone
important.

Many years later Jason Jones walked into my office in
Parma informing me one of our sub-contractors had
called him "mashuganeh." He wanted to know what it
meant. This was written for Jason after I told him
mashuganeh meant crazy or nuts, depending who was
speaking and who was receiving.

The Yiddish "F" Words

Famished – *(confused)* when the vice president CFO
(your boss) calls you into his office during lunch hour,
shuts the door, the shows you his new black camisole
with garter belt he has on under his clothes by
unbuttoning his dress shirt and pulling up one of his pant
legs revealing fishnet stockings. (true story, another
book)

Fashimilled – (covered with fungus) or how your head
feels in the morning, after you've been drinking all night,
i.e. you fell asleep in the forest without a compass (see
fablongit).

Fadreit – (turned around) or your face is facing forward and your brain is facing backward. You know when you're three and your older brother starts spinning you around while all the other siblings clap and cheer; you are so cute till you fall over.

Fakacked – (covered in dung) how you feel after you've been cleaning up dog poop in your backyard from six chows because you couldn't bring yourself to sell the puppies – Rachel, Rebecca, and Benjamin. No one could take as good care of them as you – or maybe that's just foolish in English.

Famacht – (closed) you drive forever with the map light on (of course there's enough gas to go another 10 miles) and when you finally arrive at the Texaco (where you have a credit card you can use), the light is on but the station closed at 11 pm and it's 11:09.

Fablongit – (lost) lost in the forest without a compass. Need I say more?

Faklemped – (full of pride) when you spend five hours trying to teach your new puppy how to pee outside in the yard, you have pieces of cut up hotdogs in your wet pocket, the puppy finally gets it, and you can go inside and change your pants.

20. A ROCK SLICE

On my desk is a plastic baby doll dressed in pink and a large glass jar with a lid. In its former life on my desk at work, the jar held trail mix of raisins, walnuts, almonds, brazil nuts, and sunflower seeds for visitors; now it holds treasures of shells, sand, notes, and rocks. It also holds two prized possessions – an orange rind rose and a rock slice.

When you are veterans of a Holocaust, have been homeless for most of your teenage years and twenties, stuff and money matter most. They matter more than shelter or food, because stuff can be traded for food and money buys food. My childhood home was one where money, material items (stuff), and food mattered. Mostly we believed they mattered more than we did. Our parents argued about everything; even the plastic covered couch and who had the right to sit on it.

I spent my childhood learning how to become a "success" and being "a good girl." I have a very different idea of what that means to me now than what it did then. From my teens on, I spent my time trying to succeed at becoming financially and materially successful according to the values of my parents, which meant education, nice car, good job, great house, money in the bank. The American Dream personified.

In 1992, there was a recession that hit Southern California harder than any earthquake I have lived through. I lost everything of material value – my job, my house, and all my stuff. Everything I had worked for my entire life, with very few options (or so I thought then), and very little money left. California became a bad dream as I moved near my family in Phoenix, Arizona. Probably should mention here that I married in 1967, to escape Phoenix and the family, so having to come back divorced and broke was a fate worse than prison or death (one and the same in my book).

One day, contemplating my financial failures with daily reminders from the family, I wandered into Van's Rock Shop on 7th Street in Phoenix for lack of a job or anything better to do with my time than write or listen to them. I must have looked like death walking, wandering up and down the aisles of this block long store picking up various colored rocks.

A young female clerk came over and tapped me on the shoulder. I thought she was going to ask me if I needed help. When I turned she handed me a polished rock slice – pale tan with colored concentric rings of dark rust and orange (like a slice of an old cut tree). I told her I didn't have the money to pay for it (it was $1.98).

This beautiful young woman with a sandy blond pony tail whispered, "It's a present. Remember it took millions of years of stress and pain to create something this beautiful. It's yours." I clamped my jaw shut, my eyes filled with tears ready to roll down my checks, and I nodded "thank you" to keep from sobbing.

I have a clear glass cookie jar on my desk filled with treasures. An Emily Dickinson poem, my rock slice, and orange rind rose are inside. Remember it takes millions of years of stress and pain to create things this beautiful. They're free. They're yours. May I share them with you?

21. HEART CONVERSATIONS

Yiddish was our language – my Mother and I. It was the only common language Jews spoke to each other throughout Europe. There were two dialectics – Litvak and Glitzeaner. Mom spoke one, I spoke the other. I had two names – Sarinou and Saralle (sweet Sara and little Sara). Mom and I spoke only Yiddish to each other. It was always on automatic pilot. No thought process involved. I heard her voice my brain responded in Yiddish. German was my first language, though Yiddish somehow evolved in the refugee camp when the precocious 3-year old wanted to know what all the grown-ups were whispering about. Mom died February 2006. This conversation took place at her bedside several days before her death.

Mom: *"Raialle* (her sister in Israel) *dost a bissalle perfume?"* (Raia do you have some perfume?)

Saralle: *"Vart a minute, eech ob a bisalle perfume in the car?"* (Wait a minute, I have a little perfume in the car.)

(I brought my extra bottle with me to Phoenix. How did I know to bring it with me? I never carry perfume in the car. I ran back to get it before I drove to Phoenix. That bit of ESP still eludes me.)

Saralle: *"Mom, dee vilst perfume?"* (Mom, do you want some perfume?)

Mom: *"Nu, spritz meech oon. And lipstick, dee ost a bisalle lipstick?"* (Of course, spray me on. And lipstick do have a little lipstick?)

I put lipstick on her; a beautiful bronze color. Kissed her forehead, kissed her eyes, kissed her face. She held her face up, the way a baby holds it's face when your rub lotion on. She looked a little brighter. She breathed in the attention and breathed a little easier.

Mom: "The government owes me a lot of money. And when they pay me *Saralle* (little Sara) we're going into business. You know 85 is not too old to go into business, is it? *Dee ost g'zain dain tatte?*" (Have you seen your Father? – He'd been dead since August 2005 and they had been divorced since 1976. We hadn't told her he had died. She had a stroke two years earlier and barely knew who she was. She spent most of her time speaking to her Father Herschel in a five year old Romanian voice.)

Saralle: *"Eech ob im g'zain."* (I saw him.)

Mom: *"Git, sz'nisht git ts'zain broyges."* (Good, it's not good to remain angry.)

Mom: *"Sarinou, eech gay shtarbin?"* (Sara, am I going to die?)

Saralle: "Mom, you want to die?" I responded completely taken off guard, for how are you ever prepared to lose your parents?

Mom: "*Lobin zeech klapen dem kop in deir vant!*" (Let them knock their heads into a wall. Or in the vernacular - talk to the hand.)

My knees almost gave out, while I'm trying not to laugh hysterically. I sat down next to her bed brain racing. Her body is shot. She can lift her right arm and her head a little bit, and she can talk (boy can she talk). I had a good teacher. Here she is with her body broken, though her spirit, her heart and soul are telling the angel of death to go knock his head into a wall and come and get her if he dares.

I guess if you can escape the wrath of Hitler, be homeless for seven years beginning at nineteen, bury your parents and your first born and leave your sisters behind in Uzbekistan (and all before your 25th birthday), travel thousands of miles to Munich, survive a refugee camp with rations of peanut butter, margarine, and white bread, travel by ship three months to America (the land of the free and the home of the brave) and all before your 30th birthday. What's a little dying? Living was the hard part and she did it with gusto and lots of baked goods. Her apple cake and potato kugel are the stuff of legends, ask anyone who knew her in Phoenix, Arizona but that's another story all by itself.

Had fate treated her differently, she would have been Golda Mier and Margaret Thatcher rolled into one being telling the Arabs what they could do with the Palestinians. She would not have backed down. She had a iron will. Though her body is finally at rest, her soul is right there next to all of us telling us to be better and to do better in the only way she knew how. "*Don't eat bread on Passover,*" she would say, our conscience, our angel with an attitude.

Fate may have been kinder to me. I got to finish college, get the law degree she always wanted. I got to work in manufacturing and law. Something she so wanted to do and didn't get the chance. I earned salaries she only imagined; traveled to places she wanted to go and didn't permit herself to so she could leave an inheritance to her children and grandchildren.

When your life is almost over the Angel of Death is nothing more than another milestone one has to climb before you reach the top of the mountain. I know that I have only a smidgen of her courage and her will. But that's good enough for me. If I get there, I want to sit next to her in heaven because then I know I'll be closer to God.

(This was written from Yiddish translated notes at her bedside 26 Jan 06 in Scottsdale, AZ when she was in the hospice. Nusha died a week later.)

22. A LIBRARY IN CRACOW

I belong to a Holocaust Survivors email list that travels around the globe online helping Survivors find other Survivors. More than seven years ago I received an email about a young man who wanted to start a library in Cracow, Poland and needed help filling the shelves with Jewish books. Seems he was raised Christian to save his life. Finding out as a young adult that his biological parents were Jewish, he was determined to make this happen.

As much as I love my books, I've learned to share over the years and this seemed extremely important. I boxed up a huge box of books that included my college freshman Children's Literature anthology (that was 30 years old) and my Bat Mitzvah prayer book (which was even older). Books are one of my great loves, so there were many books that had been on my shelves for many years.

It was important I told myself and left for the Post Office, almost leaving when they asked me to fill out a myriad of paperwork for custom's reasons. Never heard anything, assumed my good deed was in a black hole somewhere at the bottom of the Baltic Sea.

While casually searching Google the other night for the three blogs I've created, to see what is being sent out to the universe (by me), I came upon this website in Polish which had my name attached. Being unbelievably curious and not knowing Polish, I used Google translator. Copy, paste, click, read. Copy, paste, click, read. I had no idea what happened to my book box until now. On Google.com it says "darczyncy" and my name. The Rabbi Remuh Jewish Library was established in June 2005 and it is the only Jewish Library in Cracow open to everyone.

I am listed as a donor. Oh my God was all I could pray through all the tears. What makes this so special is my Dad Berek Nathan was born in Warsaw. His entire family — brothers, sisters, parents, aunts, uncles died in the Holocaust. He was the only living survivor. Saving himself by running to the forest while the Nazis were kicking his brother to death in the streets of Poland. He was a teenager. Berek Nathan died August 2005 at age 87. At least some of his books are back in Poland at a Jewish Library where they always belonged.

23. DANCING WITH ANGELS

Red is a color worn by others. Haven't worn red since Howard left in '92 and I moved to back to Phoenix. So I haven't a clue what made me buy a dark red Ralph Lauren shirt and tank top yesterday morning. Maybe it was the incredible sale at Dillards or I had to have one in each color as fall and winter are approaching and I'm never going to find another sale like this in my lifetime.

My friend Melinda thinks I spend too much time by myself, so she's been planning many events in hopes I'll say "yes" to one or another. Usually, I arrive a few minutes late and often leave early. Don't like crowds much and it's too hot to be outside. Let's go to La Encantada Saturday night and hear the flamenco music special event put on but GOVAC. Yeah, right, what little cigarettes have you been smoking? Jazz maybe... flamenco never! Okay, I give; I'll meet you at 6:45 p.m.

Old habits die-hard, I'm late as usual and in the back row. Another favorite place when you're pissed at life (because somehow it's to blame for passing you by) and hiding out seems like a good solution. Can't see far away, left my glasses at home (of course did I really want to come to the show?), besides who needs to see to hear. Pablo's guitar music is dynamic, tickles the soul and as much as my feet want to dance, my butt stays firmly in the tiny white folding chair. So I whisper to Melinda, I'm going to try to move closer. She rolls her eyes...been here before, she's going to bolt any minute. "Talk to you tomorrow," she whispers.

For the next hour I'm up and down like a yo-yo (probably A.D.D. in my last life). Finally, I hide behind a plant partition close to the stage where I can see and hear everything. Red is definitely the color of the evening. While the beautiful woman in the sexy long red dress is clicking her castanets and stomping her very proper low-heeled black maryjanes, a beautiful blond little girl in a long red ruffled dress with black patent leather maryjanes is mimicking her in front of the first row. The guitar music is powerful, the tall woman stomps her feet, clicks her hands, and swings her dress showing gorgeous dancer's legs. The little girl stomps her feet, clicks her fingers, swings her dress, and twirls her ruffles 'round and 'round.

I'm lost in the music, in the dancing, and in the wondering when exactly we lose the joy of twirling when everyone is looking while we are unaware of their eyes upon us. When do we become self-conscious of other's eyes and other's thoughts of our behavior? At what moment in time do we starting judging ourselves more than anyone else could ever judge us? Why does what "they" think matter? Who are the "they"? And why do they matter so much?

When exactly God, do we stop dancing, I wondered more like a prayer than a question. And what has to happen for us to twirl, to be 5 again, playing with an open heart? A chair opens up in the front row next to friends and I sneak over and sit invisibly still. OMG, I'm in the front row! The concert is almost over; maybe no one will notice I'm in the front row this close to the stage.

For all my desire to remain invisible, 80 year old Francis, 4 ft. tall, born in Spain, complete with walker and castanets comes over asking me to dance. Now I have two fears simultaneously going off in my head – do I get

up and dance with Francis in front of several hundred strangers, making a complete fool of myself or do I turn down a little old lady who can't dance without her walker or a partner in front of several hundred strangers.

I got up and danced with Francis (who survived the Spanish Civil War before age 11, making it to Ellis Island on a ship in 1940), letting her lead me all over the place. Within minutes half the audience was up dancing and twirling. More people dancing than sitting, when Francis turns to me, winks, and says, "I knew they'd all get up and dance." In the midst of all those people twirling around, it occurred to me that courage is contagious. And so is joy.

What is that saying about being very careful what you ask for? Sometimes God listens to me a lot closer than I suspect I think he does. Last night God listened to my heart, because if he had been listening to my head, he would have heard all that grumbling about last row, heat outside, and why did I leave those darn glasses at home. He would have heard my brain telling me to sit still before Melinda told me to leave cause I was driving her crazy. This time though, my heart won out, that is why God sent me two angels, one 5 and one 80 to teach me again to dance and twirl not caring who's watching.

24. DONUT HOLES

One of the difficulties of growing up with a tumultuous childhood is that you reach adulthood not quite knowing who you are. Not knowing what's right for you and how to become whole. It's as if your middle has a large hole in it, like a donut hole. It's the place where you want the person who should have filled up that hole to fill it up. Mother, Father, Sister, Brother, Friend. It's different for each of us, as different as our life experiences. As different as the people who hurt us.

Then you pick all kinds of people to enter your place of vulnerability. You demand that they fix you; you demand they fill up that space that aches. When they don't, you send them on their way, feeling ever lonelier than before they arrived. The dichotomy is that no other person can make you whole but you, yourself. It is the way it is. Everyone's hurt is a little different and most of our searching is the need to satiate that pain and fill up the donut hole.

Enter writing enter poetry. In the process of putting those succinct fragments of words on paper, on a computer screen, one surgically removes the hurts using a pencil, pen, or key instead of a scalpel. One dissects the longing, the need, the pain and begins to learn to fill the hole with words of laughter, of joy, of inspiration, of glee. Learns to fill the void with comments from around the globe and around the universe, learns to fill up the donut hole until it no longer exists.

25. WHAT PEOPLE ARE SAYING

Rachael in Mesa, Arizona - I have visited your web page a few times before and every single time I end up crying. I have this intense sense of appreciation for your words, awe at your bravery for sending them into to cosmos for all to read and a definite feeling of closeness to you. I read your poems wishing I had your talent of putting my feelings into beautiful amazing stories of the heart the way you do.

Colleen in Cairins, Australia - Sara, guess what arrived in my mail box today ? "What if...only one child remained." I am sitting here in tears. So eloquently, so honestly, so bravely ...somehow you have transcribed the hurt, bewilderment and longing of my soul. I have found within your words a new mantra by which to live my life. I am not a pin cushion.., from the poem "An only daughter".. How fabulously perfect! You could have written that for me Sara. How that poem resonates with my experience of life and my relationship with me mother. Thank you, Thank you and God Bless You ! How wonderful she was to give you to the world.

Danielle in Wilmington, Delaware - I used to be so self-conscious, about everything. Painfully shy. I always wore red - it was all over my face. I'm not sure when it happened, maybe sometime in my early thirties, but suddenly I didn't care what people thought of me.

Strangers, that is. The last insecurity to go was that around my writing, and very much thanks to you, Sara, it is now gone. It's not that I think I'm a wonderful writer - no. It's that I suddenly realized it doesn't matter. Life it too short. Dance the flamenco, kick up those heels and infect people. I think it's wonderful.

<u>Jane in Durham, North Carolina</u> - This is one of the most beautiful poetry blogs I have seen - powerful poetry and amazing art work. Each time I visit your site I find myself paused - enjoying what language can do in the presence of a skills wide as sky and deep at that canyon ride. Could feel the fearful ride and the rushing flap of the red blur headed toward the barn. At home inside her skin, this woman, I am thinking. So we readers always feel we are where we belong - even on a horse.

<u>Brandon in Columbia, Pennsylvania</u> - Sara Fryd *really* does paint with words, and here we find a palette of emotion, in all the gritty darkness of sorrow, stretched across the skein of life. She writes for her mother's voice, silenced by tragedy and guilt, to pay homage to effect we have on those we leave behind. Mother's Guilt is so powerful a poem that my mere words could never do it justice. I could feel the tears well up in my eyes as I read Happy Meal? A story of a situation I fear is way too common and very rarely ends the way this did. The poem is a commentary on compassion with all the emotion charged by first hand experience and delivered through the eyes of understanding and empathy of one simple act. The gift and the sharing help to remind us all how we should be treating each other, with kindness and love. Bravo Sara!

ABOUT THE AUTHOR

Tashkent, Uzbekistan is my birthplace. At nine months I was taken on a journey across Europe to an American refugee camp near Munich, Germany. This is where I spent my childhood. Where everyone spoke in whispers about whom they had lost to the Holocaust. No one was immune. If their families did not die in the Concentration Camps, they had loved ones buried in fields across Europe and Asia. These stories were as memorable as the places and the tears.

America is my home. In the early fifties we traveled from Bremer, Germany to the port of New Orleans, LA aboard the USMS Gen Harry Taylor. Then by train to Phoenix, AZ our ultimate destination. Language and geography are part of my DNA. I'm not sure when I fell in love with the English language, but I know language feeds my soul. Human beings who have unusual childhoods have many stories to share. I am one of those children.